Celebrate Friendship!
LisaDosSantos

BY THE LIGHT OF THE MOON

A story of kindness and friendship above the Mighty Mac

Mango Tree Press, P.O. Box 853, Mackinaw City, MI 49701
www.mangotreepress.com

ISBN 0-9708571-0-1
Library of Congress Control Number: 2001126140

MANGO TREE PRESS

Proudly written, illustrated, printed and bound in Michigan.

ACKNOWLEDGEMENTS

We are surrounded by beauty.
Thank you God
for the beautiful Straits of Mackinac.
Thank you God for the beautiful people in my life.
To my husband, Alvaro,
for having confidence in me, for your support and love.
To my big 4 year old, Andy. You inspire me everyday.
To Jen, my "little sister," for always being there.
To Renee, for trusting our friendship.
To Rose, for the kindness in your heart.
To Kate, for giving life to my words.
To Joanna, for shedding light on the mysteries of childhood.
To Denny, Bill, and Mike, three of the most genuine human beings I know.
And to you, mom and dad for helping me become me.
For the encouragement you've given me all my life.
For your hard work and sacrifice.
I pray that I can be such a dedicated parent.

Pa, I miss you…   "You ain't heard nothin' yet."

Lisa

To my Lord, for the abilities.
My husband Marc and children, for believing in me.
My family and friends who gave the extra encouraging "push" to take a chance.
To you Lisa, for making my dreams come true.

Kate

The sun shone brightly and the air was crisp that mid-summer day.

The bald eagle called Edge wanted to play.

Like all bald eagles,
Edge is strong and graceful in flight.

To witness him soar, is a glorious sight.

But Edge spends most of his day all alone perched high in a tree.

His great size makes others feel a little uneasy.

So, there sat Edge, that morning high atop the Mighty Mac.

He sat watching the ferryboats going to Mackinac Island...

...and coming back.

A flock of seagulls followed one of the boats.
Edge sighed.
He longed for that kind of friendship.
He could have just cried.

Oddly, those same gulls appeared again soon.

Something was wrong.

The seagulls circled the bridge far too long.

Eventually, Edge summoned the courage to ask,
"Excuse me dear gulls, what is at task?"

"Oh sir, it's terrible," one of them frantically said, "Mrs. Beatrice, the bat is worried out of her head."

"Her babies, they're gone.
She doesn't know where they could be. In the daylight, they're confused and they really can't see."

"We met poor Mrs. Beatrice at her Island home, the Fort.

For her babies rescue, she was devising a plan.

We told her we'd do whatever we can."

Just then Mrs. Beatrice appeared.

She was determined.

She had hope in her heart.

She must get the search off to a start.

So, the momma bat called out as Edge and the seagulls looked on.

They had no idea that a bat had a "song."

Mrs. Beatrice sang and sang. The seagulls looked between towers. The hunt for baby bats continued above the humming bridge traffic for more than two hours.

Edge stayed back. He wanted to help now.

But how?

A long morning passed.

It was after noon when the babies were finally found.

Cheers were heard from everyone all around.

"The search is complete, my babies are safe," shouted Mrs. Beatrice with glee.

"Now dear children come home with me."

But the babies couldn't let go. They were too afraid.
They couldn't fly home.
It looked like such a long way.

Then,
Edge knew exactly what to do.

"Mrs. Beatrice," he said, "I'll take your little ones home for you."
"I can help." Edge said with pride. "On the span of my wings, your babies can ride."

"We'll wait 'til it's dark and your babies feel ready. I guarantee the flight will be steady."

Mrs. Beatrice agreed.
Darkness came soon.

Edge carried the baby bats home by the light of the moon.

Safe and sound at home on Mackinac Island, momma thanked Edge again and again.

Edge simply said, "I'm glad to help a friend."

So if some night,
when the moon is bright,
you spot an eagle high above ready to soar,

look closely dear friends...

There may be baby bats aboard.

THE END